Mickey's Young Readers Library

VOLUME

4

How Pooh Got His Honey

STORY BY MARY CAREY

Activities by Thoburn Educational Enterprises, Inc.

A BANTAM BOOK

NEW YORK · TORONTO · LONDON · SYDNEY · AUCKLAND

How Pooh Got His Honey   A Bantam Book/September 1990. All rights reserved. © 1990 The Walt Disney Company. Developed by The Walt Disney Company in conjunction with Nancy Hall, Inc. This book may not be reproduced or transmitted in any form or by any means.
ISBN 0–553–05617–4
Published simultaneously in the United States and Canada. Bantam Books are published by Bantam Doubleday Dell Publishing Group, Inc. Its trademark, consisting of the words "Bantam Books" and the portrayal of a rooster, is Registered in U.S. Patent and Trademark Office and in other countries. Marca Registrada. Bantam Books 666 Fifth Avenue, New York, New York 10103.
Printed in the United States of America
0 9 8 7 6 5 4 3 2 1
A Walt Disney BOOK FOR YOUNG READERS

Winnie-the-Pooh went into his cozy kitchen. He picked up a honey pot and looked inside.

"Oh, bother!" said Pooh. "It's empty! I'm out of honey again."

At first Pooh felt sad. He felt as empty as his honey pot.

This Book Belongs to:

But then he thought of a good plan.
  "I will go to see Christopher Robin!" said Pooh.
"He is my friend, and he always has honey. He will
fill my honey pot for me."

Pooh took his honey pot and set out through the Hundred Acre Wood. He was near the bee tree when he heard someone call, "Ho, there, Pooh!"

Pooh looked down. Gopher had popped up. "Where are you going with that big jar?" asked Gopher.

"This is not just a jar," said Pooh. "Not really. It is my honey pot, and it is empty. I am taking it to Christopher Robin so he can fill it up again."

"Hah!" cried Gopher. "Wouldn't you know?"

"That's the trouble with bears!" said Gopher. "They won't work for their honey. They want someone to give it to them. Aren't you ashamed, Pooh Bear?"

Pooh did not know what to say, so he said nothing. He just stared down at his own feet.

"Go to the bee tree," said Gopher. "Get your own honey. It's what any good bear worth his honey would do."

Pooh looked up at the tree. He saw the bees buzzing in and out. "The bee place is very high," said he. "Besides, this is not a friendly tree. It has no branches to help a climbing bear."

"And what about the bees?" asked Pooh. "They will be very cross if they see me climbing their tree."

"Use your head, Pooh Bear," said Gopher. "Don't climb up the outside. Dig under the honey tree. Then climb up the inside to the bee place. The bees will never know that you are there."

With that, Gopher jumped back into his hole and
tunneled away.

"Oh, dear," said Pooh. "I know it would be
better to ask Christopher Robin for the honey. But if
I do that, Gopher will think I am a lazy bear. I do
not want Gopher to think I am lazy."

Pooh ran and got his shovel. He began to dig under the bee tree. Soon he hit a root. He could not dig any more.

"I will make a new hole in a new place," said Pooh, and he went to the other side of the tree.

Again he started to dig. Again he hit a root.

"Oh, bother!" said Pooh.

Just then Tigger came bouncing along. "Pooh Bear!" cried Tigger. "What are you doing?"

"I am digging my way under the bee tree," said Pooh. "Once I am inside the tree, I will climb up and get some honey."

"How silly!" said Tigger.

"A clever tigger would not dig!" said Tigger. "A tigger would bounce right up to the bee place. He would take the honey and bounce away again."

"But bears are not as bouncy as tiggers," said Pooh.

"That's because they won't try," said Tigger.

Tigger bounced off as Piglet and Roo came
along. They had heard Tigger talking to Pooh.

"How is a Pooh Bear supposed to bounce like a
tigger?" Pooh wondered.

"Don't worry, Pooh," said Piglet. "We can help
you bounce. We can toss you in a sheet."

"Stay there," called Roo. "I will be right back."
He ran home and got one of Kanga's sheets.

Piglet held one end of the sheet, and Roo held the other end.

Pooh got onto the sheet with his honey pot.

"One, two, three!" cried Piglet.

Piglet and Roo tossed Pooh.
"Whee!" Pooh bounced high, and higher, and
higher. "Look at me! I'm almost there!"
But suddenly Pooh was not almost there.

Pooh came down so hard that he split the sheet.
He fell through to the ground—bump!
   "Are you all right, Pooh?" asked Piglet.
   "Don't worry, Pooh," said Roo. "I will get
another sheet. We can try again."

Before Roo could run off, Owl flew down from
his tree.

"Pooh, you are going about this all wrong," said
Owl.

"I must be," agreed Pooh. "Otherwise, I would
have some honey by now."

"Forget bouncing!" said Owl. "Fly! Like this!"
Owl spread his wings and flew to the top of the
tree. He sat on a branch near the bee place. "See?"
he hooted. "Wasn't that simple? And so quick!"

"Oh yes, Owl," said Pooh. "Now while you are
up there, would you fill my honey pot?"

Owl did not hear. He was having such a good time he could not listen. "Flying," hooted Owl. "So much better than walking—or digging—or bouncing. I can't think why so few animals fly!"

"Because they have no wings," answered Pooh.

Still Owl did not hear. He flew away. That left
Pooh with his empty honey pot. Suddenly Pooh
thought of something. He thought of his kite. It was
home, behind the kitchen door.

"Perhaps this bear will fly," said Pooh, and he
ran and got the kite.

Pooh tied the kite to his back. Then he held fast
to his honey pot and ran into the wind. The wind
lifted the kite. It lifted Pooh, too. He flew far away
from Piglet and Roo.

"Oh, look at Pooh!" sang Roo. "Hooray for
Pooh! What did Pooh do? He flew! He flew!"

Rabbit was in his garden. He heard shouting and singing above him, and he looked up. Suddenly the wind died down. Suddenly Pooh was not flying. He was falling!

"Oh, dear!" cried Rabbit. "Oh me! Oh my!"

Rabbit jumped out of the way. BUMP! Pooh came down in the middle of Rabbit's garden.

"Well, I hope you're pleased with yourself, Pooh Bear!" scolded Rabbit. "The very idea! Flying! Bears are not supposed to fly! You know that!"

"I just wanted to get some honey from the bee tree," Pooh explained.

"Honey, indeed!" said Rabbit. "If I needed honey, which I don't, I would not go to the bees. I would make the bees come to me."

"You would?" asked Pooh. "How would you do that?"

"See those bees?" asked Rabbit. "They gather their honey from the flowers. If I wanted honey, I would plant a flower garden. When the bees came to my flowers, I would take their honey. That would be much better than ruining other people's gardens."

When Piglet and Roo finally caught up to Pooh, he told them what Rabbit had said.

"That might work," said Roo.

"It might," said Pooh.

But Pooh knew he could not wait for a garden to grow. He was too hungry. He, Piglet, and Roo ran to the woods and picked lots and lots of flowers.

They took the flowers to Pooh's house. They put
the flowers into a washtub, a teacup, and some of
Pooh's honey pots. Then the three friends sat down
to wait for the bees.

Soon the bees came buzzing along. They
buzzed to the flowers. Then they buzzed to Pooh
and Piglet and Roo. One bee landed on Roo's ear.
"Oooh!" said Roo.

One bee buzzed around Piglet's head. It landed on his nose.

"It tickles!" cried Piglet.

"Don't move!" said Pooh. "Tickles don't hurt, but stings do!"

"Don't talk about stings," cried Piglet. "You are giving this bee unfriendly ideas."

"Don't worry, Piglet," said Pooh. "Now that I think of it, I am sure these are the sort of bees that do not sting!"

Just as Pooh said this, a very big bee flew down his shirt.

Pooh itched and twitched. He tried to reach down his back. He wiggled and jiggled. The bee buzzed out the bottom of his shirt.

Pooh ran. Piglet ran, too. So did Roo.

A moment later, Christopher Robin came down the path. He saw Pooh and Piglet and Roo hiding in a prickly bush. "What's the matter, Pooh?" asked Christopher Robin. "Why are you hiding there? And what are all these flowers doing here?"

"I need some honey," said Pooh. "Gopher told me to tunnel under the bee tree for it. Tigger said I should bounce up to the bee place. Owl wanted me to fly. But Rabbit said I must make the bees come to me. The bees did come," continued Pooh. "But they didn't leave any honey!"

"Silly old bear!" said Christopher Robin. "What did you do the last time you wanted honey?"

"I asked you for some," said Pooh. "I was going to do that. But then Gopher said I was a lazy bear. And Tigger said I wasn't trying."

"So you wanted to please Gopher," said Christopher Robin. "You wanted to please everyone, didn't you?"

"I did," said Pooh. "But instead I wound up
pleasing no one, and I didn't get any honey. Next
time, I will follow my own plan first."

"You can follow it now," said Christopher Robin.
He took Pooh home, and he filled Pooh's honey pot.
He made some cocoa for Pooh, too. It was lovely
cocoa. It had marshmallows in it.

Pooh and Christopher Robin asked all their friends to share the cocoa. Rabbit and Owl came. Kanga came. So did Roo. Eeyore came, and Tigger, too.

When everyone was there, Roo sang his song.
"Hooray for Pooh! What did Pooh do?
"He really flew! Three cheers for Pooh."
Everyone clapped. Why not? For just a moment it had come true. Pooh flew!

Think About It

Pooh's Friends

Can you name Pooh's friends? Explain how each
one tried to help Pooh get some honey.

After your child does the activities in this book, refer to the
Young Readers Guide for the answers to these activities and for
additional games, activities, and ideas.

What's the Story?

See how many of these questions about the story you can answer.

1. Why did Pooh need to get more honey?
2. How did Pooh try to get the honey?
3. How did Pooh finally get his honey?
4. What did Pooh learn by the end of the story?

Fun With Words

Up, Down, And All Around

Look carefully at the picture and answer the questions below.

Who is flying *over* Roo?

Who is standing *under* Pooh?

Point to the bee buzzing *in* the bee place.

Point to the bee buzzing *out* of the bee place.

Name the thing that Pooh is flying *by*.

Who is *up* at the top of the tree?

Who is *down* at the bottom of the tree?

Who has a bee *on* his nose?

What is flying *above* Pooh?

Who is flying *below* the bird?

Honey-Pot Word Search

Help Pooh find the 10 words in the Clue Box
that are hidden on his honey pot. Hint: Trace the
letters from left to right and top to bottom.

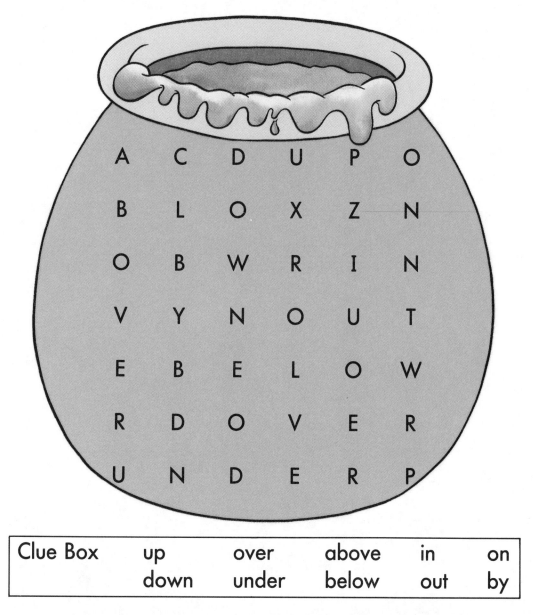

A	C	D	U	P	O
B	L	O	X	Z	N
O	B	W	R	I	N
V	Y	N	O	U	T
E	B	E	L	O	W
R	R	D	O	V	E	R
U	N	D	E	R	P

Clue Box	up	over	above	in	on
	down	under	below	out	by